Little Rabbit
and the
MEANEST MOTHER
on
EARTH

KATE KLISE

ILLUSTRATED BY

M. SARAH KLISE

HARCOURT CHILDREN'S BOOKS
Houghton Mifflin Harcourt
Boston New York 2010

Harcourt Children's Books is an imprint of
Houghton Mifflin Harcourt Publishing Company.
www.hmhbooks.com

The illustrations in this book were done in acrylic on Bristol board.
The text type was set in Brioso Pro.
The display type was created by M. Sarah Klise.

Library of Congress Cataloging-in-Publication Data
Klise, Kate.
Little Rabbit and The Meanest Mother on Earth/Kate Klise;
illustrated by M. Sarah Klise.
p. cm.
Summary: Upset that his mother will not let him go out until he cleans
his playroom, Little Rabbit sneaks away to join the circus and sells tickets
by promising the audience a view of the Meanest Mother on Earth.
[1. Mother and child—Fiction. 2. Circus—Fiction. 3. Cleanliness—
Fiction. 4. Orderliness—Fiction. 5. Behavior—Fiction. 6. Rabbits—
Fiction.] I. Klise, M. Sarah, ill. II. Title.
PZ7.K684Lip 2010
[E]–dc22   2007034404
ISBN 978-0-15-206201-9

Printed in Singapore
TWP 10 9 8 7 6 5 4 3 2
4500229051

To our mother, Marjorie Klise,
and mothers everywhere

Little Rabbit heard the drums beating far away. It could mean only one thing.

"The circus is in town!
The circus is in town!" Little
Rabbit cheered.

He watched as the performers paraded past his playroom window.

"Can I go to the circus?" Little Rabbit asked his mother.

"Of course," said Mother Rabbit. "If your playroom is clean."

"I'll clean my playroom tomorrow," Little Rabbit promised.

"I'd like you to clean your playroom now," Mother Rabbit said. "And then you may go to the circus."

So Little Rabbit started to clean. He began by pushing a moldy old experiment under his desk.

Then he tried to tidy up his collection of sticks and rocks. But somehow his playroom seemed to get messier, not neater.

"It's hopeless," Little Rabbit grumbled, kicking a stack of books. "I'll never get my playroom clean in time to go to the circus."

Mother Rabbit agreed. "No circus for you today, Little Rabbit."

"I *never* get to do anything fun!"
Little Rabbit yelled. "It's not *fair!* You're so
mean! I'm . . . It's . . . You're . . ."

DO NOT ENTER! I'M cleaning MY ROOM

But he was too angry to continue.
Then Little Rabbit had an idea.

He climbed out his playroom window.

"I'd like to join the circus," Little Rabbit told the ringmaster.

"What's your act, your specialty, your claim to fame?" the ringmaster demanded.

"Well," said Little Rabbit, "I have the Meanest Mother on Earth."

"Is that so?" replied the ringmaster. "If you can sell one hundred tickets to see her, you're in tonight's show."

"Come see the Meanest Mother on Earth,"
Little Rabbit sang. "She has two heads. And she
uses them to think up mean ways to punish the
small and the innocent."

"Really?" said the mother kangaroo. "I find that hard to believe."

"I can believe it," murmured the young kangaroo.

"Come to the circus and see for yourselves," said Little Rabbit. And he sold his first two tickets.

"Are you brave enough to witness the Meanest
Mother on Earth?" asked Little Rabbit. "She has two
heads. And green teeth!"

"She sounds terrifying," said the owl.

"She *is* terrifying," said Little Rabbit. "And ferocious, too. Why, if you just look at her the wrong way, she'll chop off your tail and *eat* it—in one bite."

"Oh, I have to see that!" said the skunk. "One ticket, please!"

"The Meanest Mother on Earth is appearing tonight!" Little Rabbit bellowed. "Don't miss your chance to see this Mysterious Marvel of a Maternal Monstrosity!"

By six o'clock, Little Rabbit had sold one hundred tickets.

"Good work," said the ringmaster. "Now get ready. You're on in one hour."

Little Rabbit raced home and crawled back in his playroom window. He found Mother Rabbit cleaning her room.

"I have a big surprise for you!" he said.

"You cleaned your playroom?" Mother Rabbit asked.

"Even better than that," Little Rabbit lied. "But it's a secret."

Little Rabbit tied a blindfold around Mother
Rabbit's eyes and led her to the circus.

When they arrived, the ringmaster was already
introducing them.

"And now, for our final act of the evening, I present
to you the Amazing Little Rabbit and the Meanest
Mother on Earth!"

At first the audience was silent. But then the crowd
began to growl.

"What's so terrifying about her?" asked the owl.

"You said she had two heads!" complained the young kangaroo.

"Her teeth are no greener than mine," scoffed the skunk. "I want my money back!"

"Me, too!" grunted the moose, who threw a peanut at Little Rabbit.

Soon all the animals were throwing peanuts.

"Wait!" said Mother Rabbit. "I'll show you all something guaranteed to terrify."

"You *will?*" asked Little Rabbit, burying his head in fear.

"Yes—follow me!"

Mother Rabbit led the animals
back to the Rabbits' house.

"Welcome to the Messiest Room on Earth,"
Mother Rabbit announced grandly. "Stinky socks!
Dirty rocks! An Emporium of Odiferous Oddities!
You won't believe your eyes—or your nose."

"This *is* shocking," said the skunk, sniffing a fossilized after-school snack.

"Unbelievable," opined the ox.

"After you conclude your tour of the Messiest Room on Earth, you may take anything you like as a souvenir," said Mother Rabbit. "In fact, take two. Or three."

It was almost midnight when the animals left.
"Next time, I'll clean my playroom myself."

"Yes, you will," said Mother Rabbit.
"I have no doubt about that."

That night Mother Rabbit let Little Rabbit sleep in
his playroom under a homemade circus tent.

"I'm . . . It's . . . You're not really . . ." Little Rabbit
started to say. But he was too sleepy to finish.

"I know," said Mother Rabbit. "I'm not the Meanest
Mother on Earth. I'm the luckiest."